John Taylor

Items on the Priesthood presented to the Latter Day Saints

Outlook

John Taylor

Items on the Priesthood presented to the Latter Day Saints

1. Auflage | ISBN: 978-3-73262-716-5

Erscheinungsort: Frankfurt am Main, Deutschland

Erscheinungsjahr: 2018

Outlook Verlag GmbH, Frankfurt.

John Taylor

Items on the Priesthood presented to the Latter Day Saints

Outlook

ITEMS ON THE PRIESTHOOD

PRESENTED TO

THE LATTER DAY SAINTS

BY

PRESIDENT JOHN TAYLOR

* * * *

SALT LAKE CITY, UTAH

* * * *

1899

THE FOLLOWING ITEMS ON PRIESTHOOD ARE PRESENTED

TO THE LATTER-DAY SAINTS BY PRESIDENT JOHN TAYLOR.

* * * *

As there is more or less uncertainty existing in the minds of many of the Bishops and others in regard to the proper status and authority of the Bishopric and what is denominated the "Aaronic or Levitical" Priesthood, I thought it best to lay before the brethren a general statement of the subject, as contained in the Bible and Book of Doctrine and Covenants.

With this view, I have made copious extracts from both of the above sacred records, and so arranged them that they can be readily comprehended by those who hold the Priesthood and are conversant with the holy order of God; adding only such remarks, for explanation, as the plain statements warranted; preferring to give generally the simple quotations, and to let them speak for themselves.

In the elucidation of this subject I have necessarily had to refer, more or less, to the Melchizedek Priesthood, as the two Priesthoods are inseperably united, the one with the other. I have also given a brief Scriptural synopsis of the Levitical Priesthood, as recorded in the Old Testament.

The following views have been submitted to the Council of the Twelve and have received their sanction; they were also laid before the Priesthood Meeting at the Semi-Annual Conference, held in the Assembly Hall, Salt Lake City, October 9th, A. D. 1880, and were unanimously accepted by the large body of Priesthood present on that occasion.

* * * *

THE AARONIC PRIESTHOOD.

AS CONTAINED IN THE BIBLE.

First.—The Aaronic, or Levitical Priesthood, spoken of in the revelations as being "lesser" than the Melchizedek; Aaron was made the mouthpiece of Moses, while Moses was as a God to Aaron. The Lord having called Moses to deliver Israel, the Prophet realized his weakness and plead to be excused. We quote from the Scriptures:

"And the anger of the Lord was kindled against Moses, and he said, Is not Aaron the Levite thy brother? I know that he can speak well. And also, behold, he cometh forth to meet thee: and when he seeth thee, he will be glad in his heart. And thou shalt speak unto him, and put words in his mouth: and I will be with thy mouth, and with his mouth, and will teach you what ye shall do. And he shall be thy spokesman unto the people: and he shall be, even he shall be to thee *instead of a mouth* and thou shalt be to him instead of God."—Ex. iv, 14-16.

It would seem from the foregoing that the Lord was angry with Moses, because he doubted the ability of God to sustain him and to enable him to speak: "And the Lord said unto him. Who hath made man's mouth? or who maketh the dumb, or deaf, or the seeing, or the blind? have not I the Lord? Now therefore go, and I will be with thy mouth, and teach thee what thou shalt say. And he said, O, my Lord, send, I pray thee, by the hand of *him whom* thou wilt send."—Ex. iv, 11-13.

The Lord further says: "And thou shalt take this rod in thine hand, wherewith thou shalt do signs."—Ex. iv, 17.

"And the Lord said to Aaron, Go into the wilderness to meet Moses. And he went, and met him in the Mount of God, and kissed him. And Moses told Aaron all the words of the Lord who had sent him, and all the signs which he had commanded him."—Ex. iv, 27-28.

"These are that Aaron and Moses, to whom the Lord said, Bring out the children of Israel from the land of Egypt according to their armies. These are they which spake to Pharaoh, king of Egypt, to bring out the children of Israel from Egypt: these are that Moses and Aaron."—Ex. vi, 26, 27. "And the Lord spake unto Moses and Aaron in the land of Egypt."—Ex. xii, 1.

3

It may be noticed that Aaron was with Moses, that God called him and spake to him and Moses, and that he assisted in bringing the message to Pharaoh, and was a prophet to Moses before he held the Aaronic Priesthood, or before that Priesthood known to us as the Aaronic or Levitical Priesthood was given. But it would seem also that the Lord spake to Aaron himself;—how and on what principle? The Lord also said to Moses, "I will be with thy mouth, and with his mouth, and will teach you what ye shall do." And Aaron spake all the words which the Lord had spoken unto Moses, and did the signs in the sight of the people. The Lord had before spoken to Moses on this subject; he now spake to Aaron. Hence Paul says, "No man taketh this honor unto himself: but he that is called of God as was Aaron." What did the Lord say to him? "Go into the wilderness to meet Moses." And then Moses told Aaron all the words of the Lord, who had sent him. Moses was thus his instructor and guide, or in other words, acted as a God to him. Thus, Aaron being selected to assist Moses and to be his mouthpiece, went with him to Egypt, and was with him in his intercourse with Pharaoh, and in the deliverance of the children of Israel from Egypt. But Moses always took the lead, and when Moses' father-in-law, Jethro, met him, "Moses sat to judge the people [not Aaron]: and the people stood by Moses, from the morning unto the evening." And when Jethro saw the excessive labors of Moses, he counseled him, If *God should command him* to choose able men to be rulers of thousands, of hundreds, of fifties, and of tens; to judge the smaller cases, while Moses should have charge of the most important. Thus Moses, and not Aaron, was the most prominent personage in these matters.

We further find that Aaron was permitted to go up to Mount Sinai. "And the Lord said unto him [Moses], Away, get thee down, and thou shalt come up, thou, and Aaron with thee: but let not the Priests and the people break through to come up unto the Lord, lest he break forth upon them."—Ex. xix, 24. It may be here asked, Who were these Priests? for the Aaronic Priesthood, as we know it, was not then introduced. But Moses was his leader, and it was he who obtained the word of the Lord, and it was he with whom the Lord conversed. For we find, "And Moses went up unto God, and the Lord called unto him out of the mountain, saying, Thus shalt thou say to the house of Jacob, and tell the children of Israel. * * * And the Lord came down upon Mount Sinai, on the top of the mount: and the Lord called Moses up to the top of the mount; and Moses went up. And the Lord said unto Moses, Go down, charge the people lest they break through unto the Lord to gaze, and many of them perish."—Ex. xix, 3, 20, 21. Moses always took the lead: "And he said unto Moses, Come up unto the Lord, thou, and Aaron, Nadab, and Abihu, and seventy of the Elders of Israel; and worship ye afar off. And Moses alone shall come near the Lord: but they shall not come nigh; neither shall the people go up with him."—Ex. xxiv, I, 2. They *saw God* and did eat and drink: "And upon the nobles of the children of Israel he laid not his hand: also they saw God, and did eat and drink." (v. 11.) And afterwards Moses was with the Lord forty days. "And Moses went into the midst of the cloud, and gat him up into the mount: and Moses was in the mount forty days and forty nights." (v. 18.) By what power did Aaron see God? May we not suppose it was by the power of the Melchizedek Priesthood? for without that no man can see the face of God and live. It, the Melchizedek, holds the keys of the mysteries of the Kingdom, even the key of the knowledge of God. (Doc. and Cov., sec. 84, p. 290.) Moses had these keys; but Aaron also saw God, as well as the seventy Elders of Israel, and the people saw his glory and heard his voice.— Ex. xx, 22; Deut. iv, 36.

It would seem that Aaron and the seventy Elders of Israel then had the Melchizedek Priesthood, and the Aaronic was about being combined with it, as we have them now. Moses held the keys of the Melchizedek Priesthood, and presided over the whole. Aaron was then in possession of the Melchizedek Priesthood; but another or lesser Priesthood was about to be conferred upon him, which was done soon after. We quote, "And take thou unto thee Aaron thy brother, and his sons with him, from among the children of Israel, that he may minister unto me in the Priest's office, even Aaron, Nadab and Abihu, Eleazar and Ithamar, Aaron's sons. And thou shalt make holy garments for Aaron thy brother, for glory and for beauty."—Ex. xxviii, 1, 2.

Does it not seem probable that Aaron, when he received this lesser Priesthood, was in the same position (as to Priesthood) that our Presiding Bishop is, holding the Melchizedek and lesser Priesthoods, but presiding over the latter, and Moses presiding over all—the Melchizedek as well as the Aaronic or Levitical, the latter being an appendage to the former? For we read that the law was added because of transgression; added to what? Was there anything but the Gospel to add it to? The children of Israel, at this time, had the Gospel and the pattern of the ark, and the commandments were given under its auspices. And the Lord spake unto Moses, saying, "And look that thou make them after their pattern, which was shewed thee in the mount."— Ex. xxv, 40. (See also the whole chapter.) And further, the words of the Lord, the book of the covenant or law of the Lord were given under the Gospel. (See Ex. xxiv, 1-8.) And the sacrifices and burnt offerings were also performed under the Gospel; and as the great Presiding High Priest, Moses, gave directions concerning the sacrifices, and himself sprinkled half of the blood upon the altar, and put half into basins, hence we have the following:

"And Moses took half of the blood, and put it in basins; and half of the blood

5

he sprinkled on the altar. And he took the book of the covenant, and read in the audience of the people: and they said, All the Lord hath said will we do, and be obedient. And Moses took the blood, and sprinkled it on the people, and said. Behold the blood of the covenant, which the Lord hath made with you concerning all these words."—Ex. xxiv, 6-8. Moses was with the Lord forty days in the mount receiving these things, viz., the laws and covenants, the pattern of the ark and tabernacle, and the tables. (See Ex. xxiv to xxxii.)

We here have a statement of the manner in which Aaron and his sons were set apart to administer in the Aaronic Priest's office, while yet under the Gospel; for we read, "And Aaron and his sons thou shalt bring unto the door of the tabernacle of the congregation, and shalt wash them with water. And thou shalt take the garments, and put upon Aaron the coat, and the robe of the ephod, and the ephod, and the breastplate, and gird him with the curious girdle of the ephod: and thou shalt put the mitre upon his head, and put the holy crown upon the mitre. Then shalt thou take the anointing oil, and pour it upon his head, and anoint him. And thou shalt bring his sons, and put coats upon them. And thou shalt gird them with the girdles, Aaron and his sons, and put the bonnets on them: and the *Priests office shall be theirs for a perpetual statute:* and THOU shalt consecrate Aaron and his sons." Ex. xxix, 4-9.

Further, "And thou shalt anoint them, as thou didst anoint their father, that they may minister unto me in the Priest's office: for their anointing shall surely be *an everlasting Priesthood throughout their generations.*"—Ex. xl, 15. We find that in all this Moses was the chief actor. Sometime after, for certain reasons specified, Aaron was to be gathered to his people, and not be permitted to enter the land, as stated. "Aaron shall be gathered unto his people: for he shall not enter into the land which I have given unto the children of Israel, because ye rebelled against my word at the water of Meribah. Take Aaron and Eleazar his son, and bring them up unto Mount Hor: and strip Aaron of his garments, and put them upon Eleazar his son: and Aaron shall be gathered unto his people, and shall die there. And Moses did as the Lord commanded: and they went up into Mount Hor in the sight of all the congregation. And Moses stripped Aaron of his garments, and put them upon Eleazar his son; and Aaron died there in the top of the mount: and Moses and Eleazar came down from the mount."—Num. xx, 24-28.

What the sin was that Moses and Aaron committed does not distinctly appear, except it was in taking glory to themselves instead of giving God the glory. For God had commanded Moses to take the rod, he and Aaron, and smite the rock, which he did. In doing this, however, Moses said: "Hear now, ye rebels: must we fetch you water out of this rock? * * * And the Lord spake unto Moses and Aaron, Because ye believed me not, to sanctify me in the eyes of the children of Israel, therefore ye shall not bring this congregation into the land which I have given them."—Num. xx, 10-12. This is the water of Meribah (or strife) because the children of Israel strove with the Lord and he was sanctified in them. David, in referring to this, says: "They angered him also at the waters of strife, so that it went ill with Moses for their sakes: because they provoked his spirit, so that he spake unadvisedly with his lips."—Psalm cvi, 32, 33.

The same judgment afterwards overtook Moses, and also for the same reason. For, "The Lord said unto Moses, get thee up into this mount Abarim, and see the land which I have given unto the children of Israel. And when thou hast seen it, thou also shalt be gathered unto thy people, as Aaron thy brother was gathered. For ye rebelled against my commandment in the desert of Zin, in the strife of the congregation, to sanctify me at the water before their eyes, that is the water of Meribah, in Kadesh, in the wilderness of Zin."—Num. xxvii, 12-14. Deut. xxxii, 48-52.

Moses plead with the Lord to have this sentence reversed, but the Lord would not grant his prayer. He said "I pray thee, let me go over, and see the good land that is beyond Jordan, that goodly mountain, and Lebanon. But the Lord was wroth with me for your sakes, and would not hear me: and the Lord said unto me. Let it suffice thee; speak no more unto me of this matter. Get thee up into the top of Pisgah, and lift up thine eyes westward, and northward, and southward, and eastward, and behold it with thine eye; for thou shalt not go over this Jordan."—Deut. iii, 25-27. And when Moses found that the Lord would not permit him to go to the goodly land, he still felt interested about the welfare of the people. For we read: "And Moses spake unto the Lord, saying, Let the Lord, the God of the spirits of all flesh, set a man over the congregation, which may go out before them, and which may go in before them, and which may lead them out, and which may bring them in; that the congregation of the Lord be not as sheep which have no shepherd. And the Lord said unto Moses, Take thee Joshua, the son of Nun, a man in whom is the spirit, and lay thine hand upon him; and set him before Eleazer the Priest, and before all the congregation; and give him a charge in their sight. And thou shalt put *some* of thine honor upon him, that all the congregation of the children of Israel may be obedient. And he shall stand before Eleazar the Priest, who shall ask counsel for him after the judgment of Urim before the Lord: at his word shall they go out, and at his word they shall come in, *both* he, and all the children of Israel with him, even all the congregation. And Moses did as the Lord commanded him: and he took Joshua, and set him before Eleazar the Priest, and before all the congregation: and he laid his hands upon him, and gave him a charge, as the Lord commanded by the hand of Moses."—Num. xxvii, 15-23.

In his day Moses was the law-giver and leader of the children of Israel. When he died some of Moses' honor was conferred upon Joshua, not all; Joshua then was to be under the priestly direction of Eleazar, the son of Aaron, who was to ask counsel for him after the judgment of Urim. Thus the lesser Priesthood began to bear rule in the person of Eleazar, the son of Aaron, although in operation it did not bear rule in Aaron's time. And while the keys and powers of the Melchizedek Priesthood were withdrawn in the person of Moses, the Aaronic Priesthood was maintained in all its powers in the person of Eleazar. Joshua indeed led the people, but had not the gifts and powers of the Priesthood which Moses had, holding indeed the Melchizedek Priesthood, but possessing only *some of Moses' honor.*

Moses died, according to the chronological record of the Bible, in the year B. C. 1451. Upwards of three hundred years afterwards we find Eli officiating as Priest; and although he was a good man, he did not control his sons, nor stop their iniquitous practices; for which he and his sons were reproved by the Lord. And Samuel took his place, and he selected and anointed Saul, who had, as Joshua, part of Moses' honor. And the Aaronic Priesthood continued to exercise its priestly power, more or less, until Christ; of which as appears John was the *last legitimate High Priest.*

In the new translation the removal of the Melchizedek Priesthood is clearly defined as follows: "And the Lord said unto Moses: Hew thee two other tables of stone, like unto the first, and I will write upon them also, the words of the law, according as they were written at first on the tables which thou brakest: but it shall not be according to the first, for I will take away the priesthood out of their midst; therefore my holy order [or the Melchizedek], and the ordinances thereof, shall not go before them; for my presence shall not go up in their midst, lest I destroy them. But I will give unto them the law as at the first, but it shall be after the law of a carnal commandment; for I have sworn in my wrath, that they shall not enter into my presence, into my rest, in the days of their pilgrimage."—Ex. xxxiv, 1, 2.

The Lord said unto Moses: "Thou canst not see my face at this time, lest mine anger is kindled against thee also, and I destroy thee and thy people; for there shall no man among them see me at this time and live; for they are exceeding sinful. And no sinful man hath at any time; neither shall there be any sinful man at any time, that shall see my face and live."—N. T. Ex. xxxiii, 20. He did, however, place him in the cleft of a rock, and covered him with His hand, and permitted him to see His back parts; but not His face. A little while before this, Moses and Aaron, Nadab and Abihu, and seventy of the Elders of Israel saw God, and did eat and drink.—Ex. xxiv, 9-11. But now Moses even, could not see his face, nor any of the people go near him, and when Moses had been a second time on the mount and his face shone so that they could not look upon him, Moses had to put a vail on his face.—Ex. xxxiv, 29-35.

Paul in referring to this says: "And not as Moses, which put a vail over his face, that the children of Israel could not steadfastly look to the end of that which is abolished: but their minds were blinded; for until this day remaineth the same veil untaken away in the reading of the Old Testament; which vail is done away in Christ. But even unto this day, when Moses is read, the vail is upon their heart. Nevertheless when it shall turn to the Lord, the vail shall be taken away."—II. Cor. iii, 13-16.

From the foregoing and from the whole history of the Aaronic Priesthood until the coming of Christ, it appears that, with the exception of some prominent prophets who held the Melchizedek Priesthood, as the direct gift of God, without, it would seem, the power to confer it upon others—not having an organization—there was very little of the manifestation of the gift and power of God among the people of the Jews, so that it might truly be said, "There arose not a prophet since in Israel like unto Moses, whom the Lord knew face to face, in all the signs and the wonders which the Lord sent him to do in the land of Egypt, to Pharaoh, and to all his servants, and to all his land; and in all that mighty hand, and in all that great terror, which Moses showed in the sight of all Israel."—Deut. xxxiv, 10-12.

From the foregoing it is evident:

First.—That the Melchizedek Priesthood was greater than the Aaronic, and that while it ruled, it controlled all matters pertaining to the government and instruction of the people, and that it organized and directed the Aaronic Priesthood, which was in reality an appendage to the greater.

Second.—That when the Melchizedek Priesthood was in a great measure withdrawn, as there was no regular organization of that Priesthood, it was left to a great extent to the guidance and direction of the Lord, who, from time to time, inspired different men as Prophets, who came to the people with the word of the Lord, receiving their inspiration and calling directly from him, as Ezekiel, Isaiah, Jeremiah, Daniel and others. But that a portion of Moses' spirit rested upon Joshua, upon the seventy Elders of Israel, upon the Prophets in the days of Elijah, Elisha and others.

Third.—That the Aaronic Priesthood continued in its full force, having a complete organization, which it received under the hands of Moses, or through the Melchizedek Priesthood.

Fourth.—That the Aaronic Priesthood, being continued, it held the Urim and Thummim, and gave direction to Joshua, who was set apart by Moses, and to Saul, David, Solomon and others, who were anointed and set apart to their

9

kingly power, and to rule over and to lead and direct Israel, and that this state of things continued until Christ. The High Priests of the Aaronic Priesthood being the acknowledged representatives of God, holding the priestly power: whilst the kings were anointed by them, or by their priestly authority, and the kings and rulers had to get the word of the Lord from the Aaronic Priesthood, or through the Urim and Thummim.

Fifth.—It is further evident that this Priesthood became, in many instances, very corrupt, and incurred the displeasure of God, and that many of the kings also, though anointed, perverted their office and calling, and instead of being the protectors and saviors of Israel, helped to lead them astray.

Sixth.—It is evident that all the Aaronic Priesthood did not have the Urim and Thummim, nor did they call, anoint and direct kings, or bear rule in the nation. But only the High Priest—one man—and that one man presided over and directed the action of the kings, telling them when to go out to war, and when not to go, and giving unto them the word of the Lord through the Urim and Thummim.

Seventh.—That they only had one tabernacle, one ark of the covenant, or one temple at one time; and not as we, many stakes, many temples, and many services. But then they, when Moses left, were under the Aaronic, and we are under the Melchizedek Priesthood; they were under the law and the Mosaic dispensation; we are under the Gospel, and in the dispensation of the fullness of time, and have consequently labors and duties to perform which did not belong to them.

It may be proper here to remark that there was a council, called a "senate of the children of Israel."—Acts v, 21. The High Priest called this council together. The council, it is said, was composed of seventy men or judges, and to have taken its rise from the installment of the seventy Elders spoken of in Num. xi, 16, 17. They were to be known by Moses to be Elders of the people and officers over them—"Able men, such as fear God, men of truth, hating covetousness"—a portion of Moses' spirit was to be given unto them, and they were to help him to bear the burdens of the people. As Saul was anointed by Samuel to be captain over the Lord's inheritance, and the Spirit of the Lord was to come upon him, and he was to prophesy and be turned into another man. (See I. Samuel x, 6.) And God gave him another heart, and all the signs came to pass that day, and he prophesied.

This senate or council was known by the name of the Sanhedrim, and it is said, sat in the form of a half moon. This council is spoken of in John xi, 47-52. "Then gathered the Chief Priests and Pharisees a council. * * And one of them named Caiaphas, the High Priest, said * * it is expedient for us that one man should die for the people. * * And this spake he not of himself; but being

High Priest that year, he prophesied that Jesus should die for that nation, and not for that nation only; but that also he should gather together in one the children of God that were scattered abroad." "Now Caiaphas was he which gave counsel to the Jews, that it was expedient that one man should die for the people."—John xviii, 14. This council had not the power of death, (ver. 31.) (See also Acts iv, v and vi.) About this Sanhedrim there is little or nothing said in the Old Testament nor of the organization of this court. It is thought by some it existed after the captivity, or in the days of the Maccabees only.

There is another remarkable thing about the Aaronic Priesthood, or at least about the early action of Aaron, as an associate of Moses. When Moses was first called upon to deliver Israel from Egyptian bondage, he told the Lord that they would not believe him, nor hearken unto his voice, and Moses was told to cast his rod upon the ground, and it became a serpent, and he fled from before it; but when the Lord told Moses to take it by the tail, and he caught it, it became a rod again. Then the Lord told him to put his hand into his bosom, and when he took it out it was leprous. He was told to put it into his bosom again, and it was restored and like his other flesh. Still, Moses was unconvinced and said, "O my Lord, I am not eloquent, neither heretofore, nor since thou hast spoken unto thy servant; but I am slow of speech and of a slow tongue. And the Lord said unto him. Who hath made man's mouth? or who maketh the dumb, or deaf, or the seeing, or the blind? have not I the Lord? Now therefore, go, and I will be with thy mouth, and teach thee what thou shalt say."—Ex. iv, 10-12. Yet Moses was not satisfied and shrank from his mission, and said: "O my Lord, send, I pray thee, by the hand of *him* whom thou wilt send. And the anger of the Lord was kindled against Moses, and he said. Is not Aaron the Levite thy brother? I know, that he can speak well. And also, behold, he cometh forth to meet thee: and when he seeth thee, he will be glad in his heart. And thou shalt speak unto him, and put words in his mouth: and I will be with thy mouth, and with his mouth, and will teach you what ye shall do. And he shall be thy spokesman unto the people: and he shall be, even he shall be to thee instead of a mouth, and thou shalt be to him instead of God. And thou shalt take this rod in thine hand, wherewith thou shalt do signs." (See the whole of chap. iv, Ex.)

From the above it would seem that if Moses would have done as the Lord requested him, Aaron would not have been called. Moses shrank from the responsibility; and though the Lord was angry with him yet he gave unto him a helper in Aaron. A revelation through the Prophet Joseph Smith, says: "Now this Moses plainly taught to the children of Israel in the wilderness, and sought diligently to sanctify his people that they might behold the face of God; but they hardened their hearts and could not endure his presence, therefore the Lord in his wrath (for his anger was kindled against them) swore that they should not enter into his rest while in the wilderness, which rest is the fullness of his glory. Therefore he took Moses out of their midst, and the Holy Priesthood also; and the lesser Priesthood continued, which Priesthood holdeth the key of the ministering of angels and the preparatory Gospel, which Gospel is the Gospel of repentance and of baptism, and the remission of sins, and the law of carnal commandments, which the Lord in his wrath, caused to continue with the house of Aaron among the children of Israel until John, whom God raised up, being filled with the Holy Ghost from his mother's womb; for he was baptized while he was yet in his childhood, and was ordained by the angel of God at the time he was eight days old unto this power, to overthrow the kingdom of the Jews, and to make straight the way of the Lord, before the face of his people to prepare them for the coming of the Lord, in whose hand is given all power."—Doc. and Cov. Sec. 84, pars. 23-88. pp. 290-1. Again, Paul says, "If therefore perfection were by the Levitical Priesthood, (for under it the people received the law,) what further need was there that another Priest should rise after the order of Melchizedek, and not be called after the order of Aaron? For the Priesthood being changed, there is made of necessity a change also of the law."—Heb. vii, 11, 12. (See also chapters viii, ix and x.) John the Baptist came as the forerunner of Christ, and baptized him as stated. "Then cometh Jesus from Galilee to Jordan unto John, to be baptized of him. But John forbade him, saying, I have need to be baptized of thee, and comest thou to me? And Jesus answering said unto him. Suffer it to be so now: for thus it becometh us to fulfill all righteousness. Then he suffered him. And Jesus, when he was baptized, went up straightway out of the water: and lo, the heavens were opened unto him, and he saw the spirit of God descending like a dove, and lighting upon him: and lo, a voice from heaven, saying. This is my beloved Son, in whom I am well pleased."—Matt, iii, 13-17. On inquiry being made, Jesus said of John the Baptist, "Verily I say unto you, Among them that are born of women, there hath not risen a greater than John the Baptist; notwithstanding he that is least in the kingdom of heaven is greater than he."—Matt, xi, 11. Again Jesus said, "And if ye will receive it, this is Elias which was for to come. He that hath ears to hear, let him hear." (vers. 14, 15.) But they would not receive it: they beheaded John and crucified Jesus; hence the restoration, the mission of Elias was postponed until he appeared to Joseph Smith and Oliver Cowdery in the Kirtland Temple. (Doc. and Gov. Sec. ex, p. 405.) At which time Elijah came, as Malachi says: "Behold, I will send you Elijah the prophet before the coming of the great and dreadful day of the Lord: and he shall turn the heart of the fathers to the children, and the heart of the children to their fathers, lest I come and smite the earth with a curse."—Mal. iv, 5, 6.

It seems from the foregoing that Moses had the greater or Melchizedek

Priesthood; that when he was taken, the keys went with him; that the Aaronic Priesthood ruled until Christ, and the people were under the law; that when Christ came he introduced a better covenant and restored the Gospel; and that the Bishopric was, and the Aaronic Priesthood is, under the Melchizedek, and an appendage thereto, as are also all Elders appendages to the Melchizedek Priesthood; and it is also evident that the Presidency of that Priesthood presides over all, as did Melchizedek, Moses, Joseph Smith, etc., with Jesus at the head, as the great Presiding High Priest.

But if, as Paul says, the Priesthood being changed, then is made of necessity a change also of the law; or in other words, a change from the law of carnal commandments and ordinances to the law of the Gospel. Yet the Aaronic Priesthood, as the Melchizedek, is an everlasting Priesthood, as before exhibited, and continueth forever as an appendage to the Melchizedek Priesthood; and hence in the old apostolic days, when under an organization of the Melchizedek, the latter is the most prominent, and very little is said about the Levitical or Aaronic: probably on account of the peculiar traditions and superstitions of the Jews, which made it almost impossible for them to comprehend the greater or Melchizedek. Yet the Aaronic cannot be ignored, and in the dispensation of the fullness of times it again comes forth, as one of the grand aids or appendages to the Melchizedek Priesthood; and hence in the ushering in of this dispensation, John the Baptist appears on the stage and confers the Aaronic Priesthood upon Joseph Smith and Oliver Cowdery.

Having therefore traced out these two Priesthoods, principally from the old Scriptures, we how turn to the revelations given by Joseph Smith in the introduction of the Priesthood, as revealed by the Latter-day Prophet in the ushering in of the dispensation of the fullness of times.

PRINCIPALLY ON THE AARONIC PRIESTHOOD OR BISHOPRIC.

THE AARONIC PRIESTHOOD CONFERRED.

"Words of the Angel, John, (the Baptist,) spoken to Joseph Smith, Jr., and Oliver Cowdery, as he (the angel) laid his hands upon their heads and ordained them to the Aaronic Priesthood, in Harmony, Susquehanna County, Pennsylvania, May 15th, 1829:

"Upon you, my fellow servants, in the name of Messiah, I confer the Priesthood of Aaron, which holds the keys of the ministering of angels, and of the Gospel of repentance, and of baptism by immersion for the remission of sins; and this shall never be taken again from the earth, until the sons of Levi do offer again an offering unto the Lord in righteousness."—Doc. and Cov., Sec 13, p. 108.

We quote from some of the first revelations given to the Prophet Joseph Smith upon this subject. "Every President of the High Priesthood (or Presiding Elder,) Bishop, High Councilor, and High Priest, is to be ordained by the direction of a High Council or General Conference. Presiding Elders, Traveling Bishops, High Councilors, High Priests, and Elders, may have the privilege of ordaining where there is no branch of the Church."—Doc. and Cov., Sec. 20, pars. 67, 66, p. 127. At this time Presidents of the High Priesthood, Presiding Elders, Bishops, High Councilors, and High Priests were placed on the same footing. It may be observed that Traveling Bishops are here referred to. These were given for the regulation of the newly organized branches or churches.

From the above we learn: That before the appointment of Bishops there were revelations given and arrangements made for this office. Whilst the following teaches us:

That certain men among the Saints should be appointed by the voice of the Church, to look after the poor and needy, and to govern the affairs of the property of the Church. "And now I give unto the Church in these parts, a commandment that certain men among them shall be appointed, and they shall be appointed by the voice of the Church; and they shall look to the poor and the needy, and administer to their relief, that they shall not suffer; and send them forth to the place which I have commanded them."—Sec. 38, pars.

34, 35, p. 163. The place referred to at that time was Kirtland, Geauga Co., Ohio. (par. 32.)

Edward Partridge was ordained a Bishop—the first Bishop in the Church—and was called Feb. 4, 1831. He was to *spend all his time in the labors of the Church*. We quote: "And again, I have called my servant Edward Partridge, and give a commandment, that he should be appointed by the voice of the Church, and ordained a Bishop unto the Church, to leave his merchandise and to spend all his time in the labors of the Church: to see to all things as it shall be appointed unto him, in my laws in the day that I shall give them."—Sec.41, pars. 9, 10, p. 168. He was to "see to all things, as it *shall be appointed unto him, in my laws*" [Who was to give these laws?] "in the day that I shall give them."

Newel K. Whitney was the second Bishop—called *to be* a Bishop, Dec. 4, 1831. "And now, verily I say unto you, my servant Newel K. Whitney is the man who shall be appointed and ordained unto this power. Even so. Amen."—Sec. 72, par. 8, p.257. "And again, I say unto you, that my servant Edward Partridge shall stand in the office wherewith I have appointed him. And it shall come to pass, that if he transgresses, another shall be appointed in his stead. Even so. Amen."—Sec. 42, par. 10, p. 169; Feb. 9, 1831.

Property was to be consecrated for the poor, and laid before the Bishop and his counselors, who are to be two Elders or High Priests. (See sec. 42. pars. 30, 31, p. 171) The residue was to be kept in a storehouse for the poor and needy, as shall be appointed by the High Council and the Bishop and his Council and for *purchasing Church lands, building houses of worship*, building up the New Jerusalem; of course he was to act as a general Bishop of the Church, (he was not confined to a ward,) to receive and distribute property, appoint stewardships, etc. It will be perceived that the High Council then had a voice in these matters. It is written:

"And inasmuch as ye impart of your substance unto the poor ye will do it unto me, and they shall be laid before the Bishop of my Church and his Counselors, two of the Elders, or High Priests, such as he shall or has set apart for that purpose. And it shall come to pass, that after they are laid before the Bishop of my Church, and after that he has received these testimonies concerning the consecration of the properties of my Church, that they cannot be taken from the Church agreeable to my commandments; every man shall be made accountable unto me, a stewart over his own property, or that which he has received by consecration, inasmuch as is sufficient for himself and family. And again, if there shall be properties in the hands of the Church, or any individuals of it, more than is necessary for their support, after this first consecration, which is a residue to be consecrated unto the Bishop, it shall be kept to administer to those who have not, from time to time, that every man who has need may be amply supplied, and receive according to his wants. Therefore the residue shall be kept in my storehouse, to administer to the poor and the needy, as shall be appointed by the High Council of the Church, and the Bishop and his Council. And for the purpose of purchasing lands for the public benefit of the Church, and building houses of worship, and building up of the New Jerusalem which is hereafter to be revealed."—Sec. 42, pars. 31-35, PP. 171-2.

The Bishop was to receive his support, and also his Counselors, or a remuneration for services. We read: "And the Elders, or High Priests who are appointed to assist the Bishop, as Counselors in all things, are to have their families supported out of the property which is consecrated to the Bishop, for the good of the poor, and for other purposes, as before mentioned; or they are to receive a just remuneration for all their services, either a stewartship or otherwise, as may be thought best or decided by the Counselors and Bishop, and the Bishop, also, shall receive his support, or a just remuneration for all his services in the Church."—Sec. 42, pars. 71-73, P. 175. (See also p. 257.)

"And unto the Bishop of the Church, and unto such as God shall appoint and ordain to watch over the Church, and to be Elders unto the Church, are to have it given unto them to discern all those gifts."—Sec. 46, par. 27, p. 193. Certain gifts were here referred to. Not only Bishops but Elders were to have this power. We further find that Edward Partridge was to appoint unto this people their portion—every man equal, giving him a writing—and every man was to deal honestly, and be and receive alike; one Church must not use the money of another Church without making arrangements to pay it. A storehouse was to be appointed. The Bishop was to receive unto himself and family what was needed for his wants, and for those of his family. This was to be an example unto Edward, Partridge, and to all Churches.

"And let my servant, Edward Partridge, when he shall appoint a man his portion, give unto him a writing that shall secure unto him his portion. * * And let that which belongeth to this people not be taken and given unto that of another Church; wherefore, if another Church would receive money of this Church let them pay unto this Church again according as they shall agree; and this shall be done through the Bishop or the agent, which shall be appointed by the voice of the Church. And again, let the Bishop appoint a storehouse unto this Church, and let all things, both in money and in meat, which is more than is needful for the want of this people, be kept in the hands of the Bishop. And let him also reserve unto himself for his own wants, and for the wants of his family, as he shall be employed in doing this business. And thus I grant unto this people a privilege of organizing themselves according to my laws;

and I consecrate unto them this land for a little season, until I, the Lord, shall provide for them otherwise, and command them to go hence; and the hour and the day is not given unto them, wherefore let them act upon this land as for years, and this shall turn unto them for their good. Behold this shall be an example unto my servant Edward Partridge, in other places, in all Churches."—Sec. 51, pars. 4, 10-18, pp. 203, 204.

First.—From the above we find that bishops were first spoken of as early as April, 1830. (See sec. 20, p. 121.)

Second.—Certain men were to be appointed to look after the poor and administer to their relief and govern the affairs of the property of the Church. (See sec. 38, pars. 34-36, p. 163, January 2, 1831.)

Third.—Edward Partridge was called to be the first Bishop, (See sec. 41, par. 9, p. 168, February 1831,) "and to spend all his time in the labors of the Church."

Fourth.—That Newel K. Whitney was called and appointed to this office as the second Bishop of this Church.

Fifth.—After this, besides Bishops' agents, there were other Bishops appointed. George Miller was appointed to the Bishopric, and had it sealed upon his head.

"I therefore say unto you, I seal upon his head the office of a Bishopric, like unto my servant Edward Partridge, that he may receive the consecrations of mine house, that he may administer blessings upon the heads of the poor of my people, saith the Lord. Let no man despise my servant George, for he shall honor me."—Sec. 124, par. 21, p. 431.

Also, "He who is appointed to administer spiritual things, the same is worthy of his hire, even as those who are appointed to a stewardship to administer in temporal things."—Sec. 70, par. 12, p. 254.

There seems to be a difference in the duties of Bishops; Brother Miller's was to be like Edward Partridge's whose duties are distinctly marked out as follows: "And again, verily I say unto you, my servant George Miller is without guile; he may be trusted because of the integrity of his heart; and for the love which he has to my testimony I, the Lord, love him."—Sec. 124, par. 20 (see also par. 21), p. 431.

At the same time and in the same manner Vinson Knight, Samuel H. Smith, and Shadrach Roundy were appointed to preside over the Bishopric.

"And again, I say unto you, I give unto you Vinson Knight, Samuel H. Smith, and Shadrach Roundy, if he will receive it, to preside over the Bishopric; a knowledge of said Bishopric is given unto you in the Book of Doctrine and Covenants."—Sec. 124, par. 141, p. 446. Vinson Knight was a Bishop, the two others were of course his Counselors.

We find from the foregoing and from what follows that there were several kinds of Bishops, as well as Bishops' agents. Bishop Edward Partridge was appointed to preside over the Saints in Zion, to purchase lands, divide inheritances, and sit as a judge in Israel, as a general Bishop to that district of country, and he had a special agent to assist him, viz., Sidney Gilbert.

Bishop Whitney was appointed Bishop in Kirtland, Ohio, yet he had charge of all the Churches in the eastern country, as a general Bishop. Neither of these, at that time, were presiding Bishops over the Bishopric. George Miller was appointed to fill the place of Edward Partridge and officiate in the same order of Bishopric. Vinson Knight was appointed to preside over the Bishopric with Samuel H. Smith and Shadrach Roundy for counselors, and at the same time that George Miller was appointed to take the place of Edward Partridge. Then there were Alanson Ripley and others. Sidney Gilbert was to be an agent unto this Church in the place that shall be appointed by the Bishop. (Sec 53, par. 4, p. 209.)

"And let my servant Sidney Gilbert stand in the office which I have appointed him, to receive moneys, to be an agent unto the Church, to buy land in all the regions round about, inasmuch as can be in righteousness, and as wisdom shall direct. * * And again, verily I say unto you, let my servant Sidney Gilbert plant himself in this place, and establish a store, that he may sell goods *without fraud* that he may obtain money to buy lands for the good of the Saints, and that he may obtain whatsoever things the disciples may need to plant them in their inheritances."—Sec. 57, pars. 6, 8, pp. 215-16.

The Lord says Edward Partridge was also to "stand in the office which I have appointed him, to divide the Saints their inheritance, even as I have commanded; and also those whom he has appointed to assist him."—Sec. 57, par. 7, p. 215 * * "Let the Bishop and the agent make preparations for those families which have been commanded to come to this land, as soon as possible, and plant them in their inheritance."—Sec.57, par, 15, p. 216. "I have selected my servant Edward Partridge, and have appointed unto him his mission in this land; but if he repent not of his sins, which are unbelief and blindness of heart, let him take heed lest he fall. Behold his mission is given unto him, and it shall not be given again. And whoso standeth in his mission is appointed to be a judge in Israel, like as it was in ancient days, to divide the lands of the heritage of God unto his children, and to judge his people by the testimony of the just, and by the assistance of his counselors, according to the laws of the kingdom which are given by the Prophets of God; for verily I say unto you, my law shall be kept on this land. Let no man think he is ruler, but let God rule him that judgeth, according to the counsel of his own will; or, in other words him that counseleth or sitteth upon the judgment seat."—Sec. 5 8 pars. 14-20, p. 218. "Let the residue of the Elders * * hold a conference;" and Edward Partridge was empowered to direct the conference which should be held by certain Elders. (Sec. 58, pars. 61, 62, p. 222.)

"And let my servant Edward Partridge impart of the money which I have given him, a portion unto mine Elders who are commanded to return."—Sec. 60, pars. 10, 11, p. 226. If not able, they were not required to return it.

"Let my servant Newel K. Whitney retain his store, or in other words, the store yet for a little season. Nevertheless let him impart all the money which he can impart, to be sent up unto the land of Zion. Behold these things are in his own hands, let him do according to wisdom. Verily I say, let him be ordained as an agent unto the disciples that shall tarry, and let him be ordained unto this power."—Sec. 43, pars. 42-45, pp. 236-7. It would seem from the above that Bishop Whitney was not yet a Bishop when he was ordained to be an agent.

"And even the Bishop, who is a judge, and his Counselors, if they are not faithful in their stewardships, shall be condemned, and others shall be planted in their stead." Sec. 64, par. 40, p. 243.

We find from the following that Bishops must be selected from the High Priests and be set apart to the Bishopric.

"There remaineth hereafter, in the due time of the Lord, other Bishops to be set apart unto the Church, to minister even according to the first; wherefore they shall be High Priests who are worthy, and they shall be appointed by the First Presidency of the Melchizedek Priesthood, except they be literal descendants of Aaron. And if they be literal descendants of Aaron, they have a legal right to the Bishopric, if they are the first born among the sons of Aaron; for the firstborn hold the right of the *Presidency* over this Priesthood, and the *keys* or authority of the same. No man has a legal right to this office to hold the *keys* of this Priesthood, except he be a literal descendant and the firstborn of Aaron; but as a High Priest of the Melchizedek Priesthood has authority to officiate in all the lesser offices, he may officiate in the office of Bishop when no literal descendant of Aaron can be found, provided he is called, and set apart and ordained unto this power under the hands of the First Presidency of the Melchizedek Priesthood. And a literal descendant of Aaron, also, must be designated by this Presidency, and found worthy, and anointed, and ordained under the hands of this Presidency, otherwise they are not legally authorized to officiate in their Priesthood; but by virtue of the decree concerning their right of the Priesthood descending from father to son, they may claim their anointing, if at any time they can prove their lineage, or do ascertain it by revelation from the Lord under the hands of the above named Presidency. And again, no Bishop or High Priest who shall be set apart for this ministry, shall be tried or condemned for any crime, save it be before the First Presidency of the Church; and inasmuch as he is found guilty before this Presidency, by testimony that cannot be impeached, he shall be condemned."—Sec. 68, pars. 14-23, pp. 249-250.

We may here notice, as elsewhere referred to, that it is the Presidency of the Aaronic Priesthood that is above spoken of, that must be set apart by the First Presidency, and also tried by them, whether of lineal descent or High Priests. Newel K. Whitney was appointed and ordained a Bishop. (See sec. 72, par. 8, p. 257) "Let my servant Newel K. Whitney, and my servant Joseph Smith, Jr., and my servant Sidney Rigdon, sit in council with the Saints which are in Zion."—Sec. 78, par. 9, p. 281. Thus it seems that though Bishop Whitney was Bishop of Kirtland, he sat in council with the Saints which were in Zion, associated with Joseph Smith and Sidney Rigdon, thus showing that he was not a ward but a general Church Bishop.

"Therefore, verily I say unto you, that it is expedient for my servant Alam, and Ahashdah, (Newel K. Whitney,) Mahalaleel, and Pelagoram, (Sidney Rigdon,) and my servant Gazelam, (Joseph Smith,) and Horah, Olihah, (Oliver Cowdery,) and Shalemanasseh, and Mehemson, (Martin Harris,) to be bound together by a bond and covenant that cannot be broken by transgression, (*except judgment shall* immediately follow,) in your several stewardships, *to manage the affairs of the poor, and all things pertaining to the Bishopric*, both in the land of Zion and in the land of Shinehah (Kirtland.)"—Sec. 82, pars. 11, 12, p. 286.

This proves that President Joseph Smith and his Counselor Sidney Rigdon were authorized to supervise temporal matters in the Church as well as the Bishop or with him. Here the Melchizedek Priesthood is united with the Aaronic to manage the Bishopric in both lands. We continue our quotations: "Every man seeking the interest of his neighbor, and doing all things with an eye single to the glory of God."—Sec. 82, par. 19, p. 287.

"Which Abraham received the Priesthood from Melchizedek, who received it through the lineage of his fathers, even till Noah; and from Noah till Enoch, through the lineage of their fathers; and from Enoch to Abel, who was slain by the conspiracy of his brother, who received the Priesthood by the commandments of God, by the hand of his father Adam, who was the first man—which Priesthood continueth in the Church of God in all generations, and is without beginning of days or end of years. And the Lord confirmed a Priesthood also upon Aaron and his seed, throughout all their generations—

which Priesthood also continueth and abideth forever with the Priesthood, which is after the holiest order of God. And this greater Priesthood administereth the Gospel and holdeth the key of the mysteries of the Kingdom, even the key of the knowledge of God; therefore, in the ordinances thereof, the power of Godliness is manifest, and without the ordinances thereof, and the authority of the Priesthood, the power of Godliness is not manifest unto men in the flesh; for without this no man can see the face of God, even the Father, and live. Now this Moses plainly taught to the children of Israel in the wilderness, and sought diligently to sanctify his people that they might behold the face of God; but they hardened their hearts and could not endure his presence, therefore the Lord in his wrath (for his anger was kindled against them) swore that they should not enter into his rest while in the wilderness; which rest is the fullness of his glory. Therefore he took Moses out of their midst, and the Holy Priesthood also."—Sec. 84, pars. 14-25, pp. 290-1.

We have already shown that there was a Priesthood conferred upon Aaron and his seed throughout all their generations. It becomes a question what Priesthood Aaron had before he had bestowed upon him what is termed the Aaronic Priesthood, when he administered with Moses? "The greater Priesthood administereth the Gospel and holdeth the key of the mysteries of the Kingdom, even the key of the knowledge of God."

Frederick G. Williams was called and appointed a High Priest and Counselor to Joseph Smith. His call reads as follows:

"Verily, verily I say unto you, my servant Frederick G. Williams, listen to the voice of him who speaketh, to the word of the Lord your God, and hearken to the calling wherewith you are called, even to be a High Priest in my Church and a Counselor unto my servant Joseph Smith, Jr., unto whom I have given the keys of the Kingdom, *which belongeth always unto the Presidency of the High Priesthood*: therefore, verily, I acknowledge him and will bless him and also thee, inasmuch as thou art faithful in counsel, in the office which I have appointed unto you in prayer always vocally and in thy heart, in public and in private, also in thy ministry in proclaiming the Gospel in the land of the living, and among thy brethren."—Sec. 81, pars. 1-3, p. 284.

From the following we find that God took Moses from the midst of the children of Israel and also the Holy or Melchizedek Priesthood, leaving the lesser, or the Aaronic Priesthood. "Therefore, he took Moses out of their midst, and the Holy Priesthood also; and the lesser Priesthood continued, which Priesthood holdeth the key of the ministering of angels and the preparatory Gospel, which Gospel is the Gospel of repentance and of baptism, and the remission of sins, and the law of carnal commandments, which the

Lord in his wrath, caused to continue with the house of Aaron among the children of Israel until John, whom God raised up, being filled with the Holy Ghost from his mother's womb; for he was baptized while he was yet in his childhood, and was ordained by the angel of God at the time he was eight days old unto this power, to overthrow the kingdom of the Jews, and to make straight the way of the Lord before the face of his people, to prepare them for the coming of the Lord, in whose hand is given all power. And again, the *offices of Elder and Bishop* are necessary appendages belonging unto the High Priesthood." Sec. 84, pars. 25-29, p. 291. From this, it would seem that the law of carnal commandments was a curse. Paul said the law was added because of transgression. ("It was added because of transgressions, till the seed should come to whom the promise was made." Gal. iii, 19.) And that it was a yoke which neither they nor their fathers were able to bear; and that Christ came to fulfill the law and introduce the Gospel which was greater—a higher law and a greater Priesthood, viz: the Melchizedek.

Both Elders and Bishops are appendages to the High Priesthood. "And again, the offices of Teacher and Deacon are necessary appendages belonging to the lesser Priesthood." (Sec. 84, par. 30, p. 291); thus Elders and Bishops are appendages to the High Priesthood, while Teachers and Deacons are appendages to the lesser, which lesser is an appendage to the higher or Melchizedek. "Therefore, as I said concerning the sons of Moses—for the sons of Moses, and also the sons of Aaron shall offer an acceptable offering and sacrifice in the house of the Lord, which house shall be built unto the Lord in this generation, upon the consecrated spot as I have appointed."— Sec. 84, par. 31, p. 291. When both of these Priesthoods are carried out and united in their purity, the glory of the Lord will be manifested upon Mount Zion, in the Lord's house, both operating according to their callings, position and authority. For it is written, "And the sons of Moses and Aaron shall be filled with the glory of the Lord, upon Mount Zion, in the Lord's house, whose sons are ye; and also many whom I have called and sent forth to build up my Church; for whoso is faithful unto the obtaining these two Priesthoods, of which I have spoken, and the magnifying their calling are sanctified by the Spirit unto the renewing of their bodies; they become the sons of Moses and of Aaron and the seed of Abraham, and the Church and Kingdom, and the elect of God; and also all they who receive this Priesthood receiveth me, saith the Lord; for he that receiveth my servants receiveth me; and he that receiveth me receiveth my Father; and he that receiveth my Father receiveth my Father's Kingdom; therefore all that my Father hath shall be given unto him; and this is according to the oath and covenant which belongeth to the Priesthood. Therefore, all those who receive the Priesthood, receive this oath and covenant of my Father which he cannot break, neither can it be moved;

but whoso breaketh this covenant, after he hath received it, and altogether turneth therefrom, shall not have forgiveness of sins in this world nor in the world to come. And all those who come not unto this Priesthood which ye have received, which I now confirm upon you who are present this day, by mine own voice out of the heavens, and even I have given the heavenly hosts and mine angels charge concerning you."—Sec. 84, pars. 32-42, p. 292.

"And let all those who have not families, who receive moneys, send it up unto the Bishop in Zion, or unto the Bishop in Ohio, that it may be consecrated for the bringing forth of the revelations and the printing thereof, and for establishing Zion."—Sec. 84, par. 104, p. 298.

In the same revelation "unto Joseph Smith, Jun., and six Elders," it is written: "Therefore, take with you those who are ordained unto the lesser Priesthood, and send them before you to make appointments, and prepare the way, and to fill appointments that you yourselves are not able to fill. Behold, this is the way that mine Apostles, in ancient days, built up my Church unto me.[a] Also the body hath need of every member, that all may be edified together, that the system may be kept perfect."—Sec. 84, pars. 107, 108, no, p. 299.

[Footnote a: Why should not this be the way now?]

We further quote: "For the body is not one member, but many. * * And the eye cannot say unto the hand, I have no need of thee: nor again the head to the feet, I have no need of you."—I Cor. xii, 14, 21.

"And the Bishop, Newel K. Whitney, also, should travel round about and among all the Churches, searching after the poor to administer to their wants by humbling the rich and the proud; he should also employ an agent to take charge and to do his secular business as he shall direct."—Sec. 84, pars. 112, 113, p. 299. Thus High Priests, Seventies, Elders, Bishops, and all men holding the Priesthood were to be actively engaged in magnifying their Priesthood.

"It is the duty of the Lord's clerk, whom he has appointed, to keep a history, and a General Church Record of all things that transpire in Zion, and of all those who consecrate properties, and receive inheritances legally from the Bishop; and also their manner of life, their faith, and works; and also of all the apostates who apostatize after receiving their inheritances. It is contrary to the will and commandment of God, that those who receive not their inheritance by consecration, agreeably to his law, which he has given, that he may tithe his people, to prepare them against the day of vengeance and burning, should have their names enrolled with the people of God; neither is their genealogy to be kept, or to be had where it may be found on any of the records or history of the Church; their name shall not be found, neither the names of the fathers, nor the names of the children written in the book of the law of God, saith the Lord of Hosts. Yea, thus saith the still small voice, which whispereth through and pierceth all things, and often times it maketh my bones to quake while it maketh manifest, saying: And it shall come to pass that I, the Lord God, will send one mighty and strong, holding the sceptre of power in his hand, clothed with light for a covering, whose mouth shall utter words, eternal words; while his bowels shall be a fountain of truth, to set in order the house of God, and to arrange by lot the inheritances of the Saints, whose names are found, and the names of their fathers, and of their children, enrolled in the book of the law of God: while that man, who was called of God and appointed, that putteth forth his hand to steady the ark of God, shall fall by the shaft of death, like as a tree that is smitten by the vivid shaft of lightning; and all they who are not found written in the book of remembrance, shall find none inheritance in that day, but they shall be cut asunder, and their portion shall be appointed them among unbelievers, where are wailing and gnashing of teeth. These things I say not of myself; therefore, as the Lord speaketh, he will also fulfill. And they who are of the High Priesthood, whose names are not found written in the book of the law, or that are found to have apostatized, or to have been cut off from the Church; as well as the lesser Priesthood, or the members, in that day, shall not find an inheritance among the Saints of the Most High; therefore it shall be done unto them as unto the children of the Priest, as will be found in the second chapter and sixty-first and second verses of Ezra."—Sec. 85, pp. 300-2.

"And let the Bishop search diligently to obtain an agent, and let it be a man who has got riches in store, a man of God, and of strong faith, that thereby he may be enabled to discharge every debt; that the storehouse of the Lord may not be brought into disrepute before the eyes of the people."—Sec. 90, pars. 22, 23, p. 325.

"Nevertheless, I am not well pleased with many things, and I am not well pleased with my servant William E. McLellin, neither with my servant Sidney Gilbert, and the Bishop also, and others have many things to repent of; but verily I say unto you, that I, the Lord, will contend with Zion, and plead with her strong ones, and chasten her until she overcomes and is clean before me; for she shall not be removed out of her place. I, the Lord, have spoken it. Amen."—Sec. 90, pars, 35-37, p. 326.

"My servant Newel K. Whitney, also a Bishop of my Church, hath need to be chastened and set in order his family, and see that they are more diligent and concerned at home, and pray always, or they shall be removed out of their place."—Sec. 93, par. 50, p. 332.

"Therefore let my servant Newel K. Whitney take charge of the place which is named among you, upon which I design to build mine holy house; and again, let it be divided in lots according to wisdom, for the benefit of those who seek inheritances, as it shall be determined in council among you."— Sec. 96, pars. 2, 3, p. 337.

"And again, I say unto you, it is contrary to my commandment and my will, that my servant Sidney Gilbert[b] should sell my storehouse which I have appointed unto my people, into the hand of mine enemies. Let not that which I have appointed be polluted by mine enemies, by the consent of those who call themselves after my name; for this is a very sore and grievous sin against me, and against my people, in consequence of those things which I have decreed and are soon to befall the nations. Therefore, it is my will that my people should claim, and hold claim upon that which I have appointed unto them, though they should not be permitted to dwell thereon."—Sec. 101, pars. 96-99, pp. 358-9.

[Footnote b: This was the Bishop's agent.]

"There are, in the Church, two Priesthoods, namely, the Melchizedek, and Aaronic, including the Levitical Priesthood. Why the first is called the Melchizedek Priesthood is because Melchizedek was such a Great High Priest. Before his day it was called *the Holy Priesthood after the order of the Son of God*; but out of respect or reverence to the name of the Supreme Being, to avoid the too frequent repetition of his name, they, the Church, in ancient days, called that Priesthood after Melchizedek, or the Melchizedek Priesthood. *All other authorities or offices* in the Church *are appendages* to this Priesthood: but there are two divisions or grand heads—one is the Melchizedek Priesthood, and the other is the Aaronic or Levitical Priesthood. The office of an Elder comes under the Priesthood of Melchizedek. The Melchizedek Priesthood holds the right of Presidency, and has power and authority over all the offices in the Church, in all ages of the world, to administer in spiritual things. *The Presidency of the High Priesthood after the order of Melchizedek, have a right to officiate in all the offices* in the Church."—Sec. 107, pars. 1-9, pp. 383-4.

Thus the Melchizedek Priesthood holds the right of Presidency, and has power and authority over all the offices in the Church, to administer in spiritual things, while the Presidency of the High Priesthood has a right to officiate in all the offices in the Church.

"This is the duty of a Bishop who is not a literal descendant of Aaron, but has been ordained to the High Priesthood after the order of Melchizedek. Thus shall he be a judge, even a common judge among the inhabitants of Zion, or in a Stake of Zion, or in any branch of the Church where he shall be set apart unto this ministry, until the borders of Zion are enlarged, and it becomes necessary to have other Bishops or judges in Zion, or elsewhere."—Sec. 107, pars. 73-75, p. 391. (See all of this section.)

He was to be a common judge among the inhabitants of Zion, or in a Stake of Zion, or in a branch of the Church, *when he shall be set apart unto his ministry.* His Bishopric is sufficient for any of these places when set apart: and he can only fill those offices for which he is set apart. But a literal descendant of Aaron has a legal right to the Presidency of this Priesthood, to *the keys* of this ministry, to act in the office of Bishop, without Counselors, except in a case when a President of the High Priesthood is tried.

We have the following on tithing: "Verily, thus saith the Lord, I require all their surplus property to be put into the hands of the Bishop of my Church of Zion, for the building of mine house, and for the laying of the foundation of Zion, and for the Priesthood, and for the debts of the Presidency of my Church; and this shall be the beginning of the tithing of my people: and after that, those who have been thus tithed, shall pay one-tenth of all their interest annually; and this shall be a standing law unto them for ever, for my Holy Priesthood, saith the Lord. Verily I say unto you, it shall come to pass, that all those who gather unto the land of Zion shall be tithed of their surplus properties, and shall observe this law, or they shall not be found worthy to abide among you. And I say unto you, if my people observe not this law, to keep it holy, and by this law sanctify the land of Zion unto me, that my statutes and my judgments may be kept thereon, that it may be most holy, behold, verily I say unto you, it shall not be a land of Zion unto you; and this shall be an ensample unto all the Stakes of Zion. Even so. Amen."—Sec. 119, pp. 418-19.

"A revelation making known the disposition of property tithing:

"Verily, thus saith the Lord, the time is now come, that it shall be disposed of by a Council, composed of the First Presidency of my Church, and of the Bishop and his Council, and by my High Council; and by mine own voice unto them, saith the Lord. Even so. Amen."—Sec. 120, pp. 419-20.

"That when he shall finish his work, I may receive him unto myself, even as I did my servant David Patten, who is with me at this time, and also my servant Edward Partridge, and also my aged servant Joseph Smith, Sen., who sitteth with Abraham at his right hand, and blessed and holy is he, for he is mine."—Sec. 124, par. 19, p. 431.

First.—We find from the above that there are two distinctive general Priesthoods, namely, the Melchizedek and Aaronic, including the Levitical Priesthood.

26

Second.—That they are both conferred by the Lord; that both are everlasting, and administer in time and eternity.

Third.—That the Melchizedek Priesthood holds the right of Presidency, and has power and authority *over all the offices in the Church*, in all ages of the world, *to administer in spiritual things*.

Fourth.—That the second Priesthood is called the Priesthood of Aaron; because it was conferred upon Aaron and his seed throughout all their generations.

Fifth.—That the lesser Priesthood is a part of, or an appendage to the greater, or the Melchizedek Priesthood, and has power in administering outward ordinances. The lesser or Aaronic Priesthood can make appointments for the greater, in preaching, can baptize, administer the sacrament, attend to the tithing, buy lands, settle people on possessions, divide inheritances, look after the poor, take care of the properties of the Church, attend generally to temporal affairs; act as common judges in Israel, and assist in ordinances of the Temple, under the direction of the greater or Melchizedek Priesthood. They hold the keys of the ministering of angels and administer in outward ordinances, *the letter of the Gospel*, and the baptism of repentance for the remission of sins.

Sixth.—That there is a Presidency over each of these Priesthoods, both over the Melchizedek and the Aaronic.

Seventh.—That while the power of the higher, or Melchizedek is to hold the keys *of all the* spiritual *blessings of the Church*; to have the privilege of receiving the mysteries of the Kingdom of heaven, to have the heavens opened to them, to commune with the general assembly and Church of the Firstborn and to enjoy the communion and presence of God the Father, and Jesus the Mediator of the new covenant, and to preside over all the spiritual officers of the Church, yet the *Presidency* of the High Priesthood, after the order of Melchizedek, have a right to officiate in *all the offices in the Church*, both spiritual and temporal.

"Then comes the High Priesthood, which is the greatest of all; wherefore it must needs be that one be appointed of the High Priesthood to preside over the Priesthood, and he shall be called President of the High Priesthood of the Church; or, in other words, the Presiding High Priest over the High Priesthood of the Church."—Sec. 107, pars. 64-66, p. 390.

It is thus evident that this Priesthood presides over all Presidents, all Bishops, including the Presiding Bishop, over all Councils, organizations and authorities in the whole Church, in all the world.

That the Bishopric is the Presidency of the Aaronic Priesthood, which is "an *appendage* to the greater or Melchizedek Priesthood," and that no man has a legal right to hold the KEYS of the Aaronic Priesthood, which presides over all Bishops and all the lesser Priesthood, except he be a literal descendant of Aaron. But, that "as a High Priest of the Melchizedek Priesthood has authority to officiate in all the lesser offices, he may officiate in the office of Bishop" * * * if "*called, set apart and ordained unto this* power by the hands of the Presidency of the Melchizedek Priesthood."

We may here notice that John the Baptist conferred this Priesthood upon Joseph Smith, and that therefore, as he held it, he had the power to confer it upon others.

Eighth.—That there are Bishops holding different positions: Bishop Partridge was a general Bishop over the land of Zion; while Bishop Whitney was a general Bishop over the Church in Kirtland, Ohio, and also over all the eastern Churches until afterwards appointed as Presiding Bishop. That there are also ward Bishops, whose duties are confined to their several wards. That there are also Bishops' agents, such as Sidney Gilbert and others.

That the position which a Bishop holds, depends upon his calling and appointment, and that, although a man holding the Bishopric is eligible to any office in the Bishopric, yet he cannot officiate legally in any, except by selection, calling and appointment.

Ninth.—That the power and right of selecting and calling of the Presiding Bishop and general Bishops is vested in the First Presidency, who also must try those appointed by them in case of transgression, except in the case of a literal descendant of Aaron; who, if the firstborn, possesses a legal right to the keys of this Priesthood; but even he must be sanctioned and appointed by the First Presidency. This arises from the fact that the Aaronic is an appendage to the Melchizedek Priesthood.

That the Presiding Bishop, who presides over all Bishops, and all of the lesser Priesthood, should consult the First Presidency in all important matters pertaining to the Bishopric.

Tenth.—That in regard to the appointment and trial of ward Bishops, it appears that they stand in the same relationship to the Presidents of Stakes as the early Bishops did to the First Presidency, who presided over the Stake at Kirtland; but that those Presidents should consult with the First Presidency on these and other important matters, and officiate under their direction in their several Stakes.

That in regard to the office and calling of Bishops it is very much like the office and calling of High Priests. All High Priests are eligible to any office in the Church, when called, ordained and appointed to fill such office. The First Presidency are High Priests. The Twelve are High Priests, High Councilors are High Priests, Presidents of Stakes are High Priests, and all their Counselors; Bishops and their Counselors are High Priests: but it does not follow that all High Priests are First Presidents, members of the Twelve Apostles, Presidents of Stakes, High Councilors, Bishops or Bishops' Counselors, they only obtain these offices by selection and appointment from the proper source, and when not appointed to any specific calling, they are organized in a Stake quorum, under a President and Council. So although the Bishopric is eligible to fulfill any office to which they may be appointed, all are not presiding Bishops, all are not general Bishops, or special Bishops, or ward Bishops, or even Bishops' agents; they occupy their several offices, as do the High Priests, by selection, appointment, as well as ordination, and that the Presidency of the Melchizedek Priesthood presides over, calls, directs, appoints and counsels all. It is further evident that as the Melchizedek Priesthood holds the keys of all the spiritual blessings of the Church, and that the Presidency thereof has a right to officiate in all the offices of the Church, therefore that Presidency has a perfect right to direct or call, set apart and ordain Bishops, to fill any place or position in the Church that may be required for that ministry to perform in all the Stakes of Zion, or throughout the world. Thus, after going through the whole matter, we come back to a term frequently used among us: Obey counsel.

THE LEVITICAL PRIESTHOOD.

As the Levitical Priesthood is referred to in the Old Testament scriptures, as well as in the book of Doctrine and Covenants, the following quotations and remarks may throw some light upon the subject:

LEVITES AND LEVITICAL PRIESTHOOD.

"And the Lord spake unto Moses, saying: Bring the tribe of Levi near, and present them before Aaron the Priest, that they may minister unto him. And they shall keep his charge, and the charge of the whole congregation, before the tabernacle of the congregation, to do the service of the tabernacle. And they shall keep all the instruments of the tabernacle of the congregation, and the charge of the children of Israel, to do the service of the tabernacle. And thou shalt give the Levites unto Aaron and to his sons, they are wholly given unto them out of the children of Israel. And thou shalt appoint Aaron and his sons, and they shall wait on their Priest's office: and the stranger that cometh nigh shall be put to death."—Num. iii: 5, 10.

Aaron and his sons held the Aaronic Priesthood, and the Levites were given unto them to minister unto them to keep his charge, the charge of the congregation, to do the service of the tabernacle, keep the instruments of the tabernacle, and the charge of the children of Israel.

"And I, behold, I have taken the Levites from among the children of Israel instead of all the firstborn that openeth the matrix among the children of Israel; therefore the Levites shall be mine; because all the firstborn are mine; for on the day that I smote all the firstborn in the land of Egypt I hallowed unto me all the firstborn in Israel, both man and beast: mine they shall be: I am the Lord."—Num. iii, 12, 13.

All the firstborn the Lord claimed as belonging to him, because when he destroyed the firstborn of the Egyptians, he spared the firstborn of the Israelites. But the Levites were appointed to fill the place of the firstborn of all Israel, and they were commanded to be numbered, viz., all the males from a month old and upward, to assist Aaron and his sons in the service of the tabernacle; at that time there were twenty-two thousand of them. (Ibid, ver. 39.)

"And the Lord spake unto Moses, saying: Take the Levites instead of all the first born among the children of Israel, and the cattle of the Levites instead of their cattle; and the Levites shall be mine: I am the Lord." (ver. 44, 45.)

The remainder of the Israelites had to redeem their firstborn, and the money for the redemption was given by Moses to Aaron and his sons according to the word of the Lord. (ver. 50, 51.)

They seemed to have been an appendage to the Aaronic Priesthood to assist in the service of the tabernacle and other duties. Aaron and his male descendants were selected for the Priesthood, and the other Levites as assistants, or an appendage.

The Levites had forty-eight cities and their suburbs provided for them from among the possessions of the other tribes: First came by lot the children of Aaron: "And the children of Aaron the Priest, which were of the Levites, had by lot out of the tribe of Judah, and out of the tribe of Simeon, and out of the tribe of Benjamin, thirteen cities."—Josh, xxi, 4. (See the whole of the chapter for a division of cities to the remainder of the Levites, or the tribe of Levi, who were thus provided for as distinct from the other tribes.) "All the cities of the Levites within the possession of the children of Israel were forty and eight cities with their suburbs."—Josh, xxi, 41.

It may here be observed that both Moses and Aaron belonged to the tribe of Levi, and that the Levites had a tithing given to them. "And the Lord spake unto Aaron, Thou shalt have no inheritance in their land, neither shalt thou have any part among them: I am thy part and thine inheritance among the children of Israel. And, behold, I have given the children of Levi all the tenth in Israel for an inheritance, for their service which they serve, even the service of the tabernacle of the congregation."—Num. xviii, 20, 21. (See also the chapter.)

There is a peculiarity about this tithing, for while one-tenth was given to the Levites, they, the Levites, were commanded to give one-tenth of the tithe to Aaron.

"And the Lord spake unto Moses, saying. Thus speak unto the Levites, and say unto them. When ye take of the children of Israel the tithes which I have given you from them for your inheritance, then ye shall offer up an heave offering of it * * * for the Lord, even a tenth part of the tithe * * and ye shall give thereof the Lord's heave offering to Aaron the Priest." Num. xviii, 25-28.

It would seem that while the Levites were called "to do the service of the tabernacle of the congregation" (ver. 6), that the Priest's office belonged especially to Aaron and his family. The Lord, in speaking to Aaron, says, "And I, behold, I have taken your brethren the Levites from among the children of Israel: to you they are given as a gift for the Lord, to do the service of the tabernacle of the congregation."—Num. xviii, 6.

It furthermore appears that while the Levites were given to Aaron, that Aaron and his sons were to hold the Priest's office. "Therefore thou and thy sons with thee shall keep your Priest's office for everything of the altar, and within the vail; and ye shall serve: I have given your Priest's office unto you as a service of gift: and the stranger that cometh nigh shall be put to death."— Num. xviii, 7.

In the case of Korah, Dathan and Abiram, whom the earth opened and swallowed up for assuming the Priest's office, "Moses said unto Korah, hear, I pray you, ye sons of Levi: Seemeth it but a small thing unto you, that the God of Israel hath separated you from the congregation of Israel, to bring you near to himself to do the service of the tabernacle of the Lord, and to stand before the congregation to minister unto them? And he hath brought thee near to him, and all thy brethren the sons of Levi with thee: *and seek ye* the Priesthood also?"—Num. xvi, 8-10. And also the whole chapter, in which is depicted the terrible judgment of God upon them for assuming the Priest's office.

From the above it would seem—

First.—That the Levites were selected in the place of the firstborn whom the Lord called his own.

Second.—That they were given to Aaron to assist him in the minor or lesser duties of the Priesthood; but that Aaron and his sons officiated in the leading offices of the Priesthood, and not the Levites.

Third.—That there was a tithing paid to them by the whole house of Israel for their sustenance.

Fourth.—That they paid a tithe of this to Aaron.

Fifth.—That on assuming the higher duties of the Priesthood of Aaron, the judgments of God overtook them.

Sixth.—That their Priesthood was only an appendage to the Aaronic Priesthood, and not that Priesthood itself as held by Aaron and his sons.

TRANSCRIBER'S NOTES:

Where the original reads "peolpe," this edition reads "people."

Where the original reads "thh," this edition reads "the."

Where the original reads "Willaims," this edition reads "Williams."

Where the original reads "Aopostles," this edition reads "Apostles."

Where the original reads "authotities," this edition reads "authorities."

Where the original reads "too frequent repetion," this edition reads "too frequent repetition."

Where the original reads "Was there anything but the Gospel to add it to to?," this edition reads "Was there anything but the Gospel to add it to?"

A case of a quotation mark appearing without a partner has been corrected by adding the partner, after comparison with the original quoted material.